TRAPPED ON MY MIND

TRAPPED ON MY MIND

LUZ PRATT

Trapped on My Mind

This book is written to provide information and motivation to readers. Its purpose is not to render any type of psychological, legal, or professional advice of any kind. The content is the sole opinion and expression of the author, and not necessarily that of the publisher.

Copyright © 2020 by Luz Pratt.

Printed in the United States of America.

ISBN   978-1-951913-21-2   (Paperback)
ISBN   978-1-951913-22-9   (Digital)

Lettra Press books may be ordered through booksellers or by contacting:

Lettra Press LLC
30 N Gould St. Suite 4753
Sheridan, WY 82801, USA
1 303-586-1431 | info@lettrapress.com
www.lettrapress.com

INTRODUCTION

Love, death, memories, holding thoughts
Without knowing
Holding life with passion and tears
Without knowing
Remembering the good and bad, love and hate
Without knowing
No names, no past, just the present with fate
Without knowing
Passing through life, with the unknowns,
No names, just with an uncertainty tomorrow
Feelings for everything and nothing
Passion for everything and nothing
Numbness and pain
Passion and rain doesn't matter
Just breathe laugh-cry and look for a mountain and climb.

Closing eyes, now you don't see
No names, no need, for what
Nothing matters at the end
Past, present, future it's just about faith.
And everything is without knowing
Reality not sure, just live, love
And at the end you will see the top of the mountain.
Having thoughts without having them
What you see at the end of your climbing doesn't matter

Luz Pratt

The only thing that counts it's probably nothing or everything.
Don't wanting to know,
Don't wanting to talk, see or hear;
Everything and Nothing,
Destiny or not, doesn't matter
At the end is without knowing, because the unknown is better,
or just because you don't want to know.

PROLOGUE

I decide to write this book to myself and others that has been experienced disturbing moments in their lives. I had the most unpredictable and painful episode that a human being can go through. Hoping that sharing this with you, can teach us, can teach me how to make a difference, in a way how people interacts with each other and learn how to love and be compassionate and caring. However, I think all that is gone now. What you are going to read is not a fiction or love story book. It's as real as the sky.

It's a very dramatic episode that recently happens to me. We need to open our eyes and listen to the illness that might or might not, in any event might hit you badly. If I can change the perspective of how we the people see and judged reactions, then just one person can be good enough as a goal, sharing my own, sharing my mind . This is a true event that impacted many lives, mostly mine.

When you see someone, anyone: wandering while walking, talking to Itself, what do you think? What comes to your mind? Probably nothing or just stared at the person? Making fun or just ignored the situation. Yet, it's a question that probably most of us don't know how to answer, but I promise you that at the end of your reading, probably and I emphasize just probably you, me, us will be able to comprehend and learn how to react in that specific situation that you might be involved or situations that you might witness throughout the path in your life, in my life, in everybody's life.

We know so little about our mind and brain but I do know that the mind had a limit, can't take too much to handle the daily situations that we deal in a daily basis; there is multiple ways to cope in life, some people drink to forget, others use drugs and so on, to defend itself, to protect themselves. But sometimes, I will say more than we know the mind shut down, perhaps because that's the only way that we know or choose to manage that unique situation that can hurt you, whatever it is.

I was inspired to write this book for those that came out from that state of mind, because they fought and they won. They were lost and they found themselves, for all of you my lectors CONGRATULATIONS, you are strong and deserve the best of the best.

From the bottom of my heart,
this book is dedicated just for you.

Character One   Myself, Strong, caring and very open mind

Character Two   Unable to point, too many people involved that were trapped with me in my delusions.

BEGINNING

I was working out of state—to be more specific, Arizona. I was living in a nice hotel, The Residence Inn Marriott. The Arizonians were very open and talkative; I felt welcomed by them. I went to my training in this assignment, and it went well. I was excited to be starting a short-term job. It would last for about a month, so I would have new coworkers for a short period of time. By that time, my husband was again overseas, so I had chosen to travel. I didn't want to be alone anymore; there was too much of nothing and everything. So I decided to travel. In Arizona, at the beginning, while driving my car, I started asking myself, *Is this is a right move?* But I realized it was too late; I had already gone too far, and I would have to accomplish this assignment. At the beginning I didn't know the roads. I guess that's normal for my first time in Arizona. The first two to three weeks were not too different from my previous job. However, I will say that there were fewer hours of work, but my patients had different illnesses; they needed to be taken good care of; they needed to talk and be listened to. I was excited because I knew that most diseases are not properly diagnosed because people just hear but don't listen. My days went on with not too much change. I lacked sleep, as usual. I woke up every morning and started my routine: coffee, prayers, take a shower, get dressed, no breakfast—no time for that—jump in the rental car, and start my day.

Usually the days ran smoothly but were busy. I gave the best of myself with all the knowledge and love I could give. I never regretted it, but again, there was not always time to have lunch. The day ended, and I got to the car and back to the hotel, to the loneliness, the empty room, with nothing, no one there.

However, as soon I was out of the work environment, strange feelings started filling my insides. I couldn't explain what was happening. Perhaps it was the loneliness, the lack of energy, feeling drained, with no stamina at all. There was no life inside of me. I realized that I had had these feelings for years, always masking them with a smile. The patients became family in my heart. *Hi, Sir/Ma'm. How can I help you?* That was my introduction to each one of them.

In my personal life, I tried to give all of myself to my family. Those days were stressful; I needed to accomplish my mission in earth. I was living a life phase and wasn't paying too much attention to myself.

Looking back now, I realize that those feelings and thoughts were indeed in me for years. I used to say, *Tomorrow will be better; everything will feel normal.* But what is normalcy? Nobody knows. Your body keeps moving forward, but your mind goes backward, stuck without any warnings. Did I ignore or deny some signs? Or did the necessity to keep working take my last drop of energy? These are questions that I still don't have the answer to and probably never will. You can run, but you can't escape.

I lived alone for several years due to my husband's travels; my kids were growing, so I stayed behind. They grew up so fast. My life then became bizarre; I didn't know where I belonged anymore. I had no expectations, no feeling. I needed love.

The majority of my life after that was in solitude in the woods in upstate New York.

Yes, we moved from my precious island to the states. I guess that's when my life started changing, falling apart. In this new life, with new expectations, there were too many unknowns, too much of always hoping for the best.

I started a new practice, working long hours and long days, always concerned that again I didn't have enough time for my new family, much less myself. Years passed with no change in my behavior; I changed masks every day. No one noticed my feelings; everybody was so busy demanding my presence. My husband, on the other hand, traveled again and again. The eyes that I fell in love with were not as green now as I'd thought. We both had too much to hide; we were living different lives, and I did not recognize this man anymore. He was a stranger. I had no more memories; they were gone. No holding hands, I felt unloved, alone, lost. I hadn't signed up for this. Then I decided to change jobs, thinking that perhaps changes are always good, I was willing to create a new me with no more sorrows.

I decided to start doing traveling *locums tenants*, which is covering practices that are down in doctors, covering their vacations, or just needing extra help.

Another day ended and I went back to my room. There were still four weeks more to end this assignment. I continued with the same routine day after day, waking up, take a shower, get dressed, and jump in the car, always thinking, *Another day but a different challenge.* I was getting used to the surroundings already and did not have to use the GPS anymore to drive to work.

My husband decided to take a break and came to Arizona. We were together. We decided not to travel any more and to start from scratch. We wanted to create new memories; we need to start knowing each other again. However, it didn't last. He stayed with me the first two weeks, and then he went back home. I fell disappointed, but again, I went with the flow. I was feeling like a loser. My instincts were telling me that something would go wrong.

I started feeling strange, different, lost, frightened and abandoned. I wondered if perhaps this was the beginning of my death, the beginning of me getting into a dark place.

Memorial Day weekend was coming soon. I was not excited and I had no plans, so I guessed it would be me and myself again. But something continued growing inside; something strange was happening. Very gradually I started hearing voices in my head; they were very real, talking to me and about me. I thought that I might be exhausted from sleep deprivation. I knew that was not a good thing, and I was not eating well, which also might be the cause of these hallucinations. In my entire life, I have always found excuses as answers to all my concerns and issues. Denial? I always kept these thoughts just for me. I never shared them. They were probably growing deep inside me.

I do remember weird dreams. they were so vivid and real. Actually I didn't know if they were real or not. Scared, frightened, strange dreams and issues came into my mind.

I started feeling sick and knew that I had some kind of infection associated with fever, chills, and gastrointestinal symptoms that I ignored. I had to keep working, and there was no time for me. I was feeling weak and dizzy. That's when I started thinking that I should reach for help, so in my confusion, I decided to go to the hospital. The hotel called the ambulance, and they took me to the emergency room. The hospital was just walking distance from the hospital, but I did not know. They asked me questions, which I don't remember well. They did tell me that I was dehydrated, and they gave me fluids and electrolytes. I also remember that the doctor found me anxious and wanted to give me something for the anxiety. I refused it and had the urge to get out of the hospital.

When they discharged me, they offered to call a taxi, but the hotel was so close that I decided to walk, even though I had no shoes with me. You might imagine how my walking was—I could see the hotel, but it took me about three hours to get there. I kept the hallucinations to myself and did not mention them, probably because in my mind they seemed real or because I was just exhausted. Oh *God*, I wanted badly to go home. But where was home? I went to my room and decided to try to sleep or at least rest. But I couldn't; my brain was on fire; my body was numb. *Please, God, help me, give me your strength, have mercy.*

Then I decided to get up, and suddenly, I started seing nets all over the room that seemed real in my mind. They had different shapes and were all over. I wanted to touch them and was surprised when I found I was doing it. In my mind I knew that something was not right, so I tried to continue my routine. It was a long weekend.

I was in terror that I was crossing the fine line between sanity and insanity.

And things started getting worse when I began to hear voices, recognized voices of people that were part of my normal world. People who I loved. Then the scariness was getting to me. I couldn't tell what was real and what was not. I was losing it; the voices didn't stop, and what I was seeing was getting worse.

The hallucinations become constant. Some of them were very painful; others I would call eccentric in a way that, at that very moment, I did not understand, and probably that was for the best. I started walking and wandering through the hotel, again with no shoes, but it did not matter. By that time, I was already trapped in my mind. I did try to look normal to others, and I fooled myself—who can say I was behaving well?

I questioned myself: did they see and hear as well as me? That I will never know, I am pretty good at hiding my reality, my me, myself, sorrows and loneliness. In a subconscious way, I was trying to look for help. I was texting and calling people that I trusted, just hoping that one of them would sense the serious situation that I was getting into. I really wanted to see and touch someone real, not just hallucinations. The mind plays games, and I was already part of that.

I start hating the days and nights. I just wanted to sleep, but the voices of my brother and my sister-in-law were calling me, and I started walking all over the hotel and knocking on doors because the voices were coming from everywhere.

If just someone, anyone, had asked me how I felt, if I was okay, perhaps—probably—I would lie. I knew was just the beginning of my mental derangement, but did not happened. Have you ever feel caring the world in your back, your silence tells me it's a yes? Have you ever feel that you can't give anymore to no one because you know that already you are gradually getting empty? I wanted to be the one in the other side, someone that received and feel cared and loved.

The mind play in mysterious ways, there is so little that we know and understand about the mind, the brain. Mine was really playing with me. There was a moment that I did not know what was real or just my imagination; or probably everything was the true reality, was so vivid that I couldn't handle it any more.

After that day, which was a Friday, everything started falling apart, went downhill fast, my mind couldn't stop. I knew that there was no escape for me, I was scare to death but nothing I can do about it. I fought back because I knew the outcome, but I was weak and feeling frighten. During all that time no water, no food no sleep, I was TRAPPED in my mind.

I started seen my husband behind my bed, trying to put the equipment, kind of FBI equipment. With cameras that he and everyone that has the same equipment can hear me and seen me, I try to talk to him telling him that leave me alone, that I knew what he was doing, that I know that he was in the hotel, but he was just trying to hide and disappear again. The nets with shapes of animals, trees etch, were driving me to cry and I just shout out loud stop; stop. But were getting worse, I started seen them wherever I go. I try to touch the animals and yes I did indeed in my mind. Then I decide that I needed help so I call the police, yes 911 from the hotel. I was walking in the hallways and telling quietly to people that I didn't know what was happening, probably begging that someone pay attention, really listen, needed help me and call 911 again or was the hotel that made a call, don't recall, Did I was paranoid?

The police came to the hotel and search my room, looking for alcohol, drugs, or who knows. Nothing was found don't even the nets that were driving literally insane. I did not explain to the police that my room was changing constantly. I mean was like a carrousel it's hard to explain. Friday night which was the Memorial weekend, I saw a different scenario in my hotel room; was kind like a competition for be u part of a club/fraternity who knows. I saw that in the second floor of my room, which I did not have, there was this reunion of people that I never met, except two persons that I will change the names, Mike and Joe. The people that participate in the competency had to do certain things that were disgusting and actually beyond my comprehension.

Was kind of a party for rich people that were eccentric and by my judgment for what was listening and seeing with no moral at all, I don't remember well because I was trying to hide, they were trying to convince me to play, mostly Mike; but I refused even if I have to pay consequences at the end? They were doing kind of sexual games, I say that because they have to kiss someone and other things that for respect of my readers I don't want to be more explicitly just take my word. I try to sleep because I didn't want to see whatever they were doing. Meanwhile my room was changing depending of their game. Was mostly in the water. Was like a horror and hurtful movie with different phases in their game. I remember gun shots, people dying because couldn't pass the phase that they needed to accomplish to be part of that Exclusive Club.

While all these was happening, there always someone watching me, all the time and me just try to ran away from that nightmare.

Actually if I try to describe that world that was in my mind, I will not be able to do it. That memory was very painfully, confused and disturbed. You my lectors will understand that, and for that I thankful. Memories that probably are blocked as a defense, each episode was created by the dark side, therefore I will not remember what hurts the most.

I guess that I slept on and off just wake up when the get together was almost one, Mike was always asking how I was doing, apparently he was kind of ashamed and did not want to talk to me. The shooting was over. Never figure out what truly was happening. I do hear that will be a big get together for the ones that pass all the phases of that club or fraternity. I was so confused and mad about the situation. The following day I was feeling more disturbed and confused. Didn't know what was real or not. I remembered that I start praying, still have one week more in my assignment. Did I will be able to do it?

Memorial day come I knew that I will not be able to go back to work, However I try to go and walked to the car, but I fell and hit the back of my head, crawling to the lobby, I collapsed again and the ambulance and the police took me again to the emergency room. Yes, they convinced me to go to the hospital. Was a very bad experience I heard their laughing, no compassion, joking about my hallucinations. I answer all their questions during the episode. I heard the words crazy, alcohol, drugs. I wanted to scream bul I knew that then they will not let me go from the Hospital. I want to get out of the hospital, but I wasn't allowed, they baker act me, for my safety. Safety of what? I was already in danger, my cognitive was gone, what is right or wrong? Finally, I convinced the doctor, told him the truth, I will be flying back home in less than 48 hours, they let me go. But why they didn't medicate me with something, my head is ready to explode, they had less cognition than me? It's just a matter of common sense; here is this lady very anxious, that will fly alone? Let's protect her with something mild until she gets home? Didn't happen, why I didn't ask? Perhaps I don't want them to think that I was looking for pills, that's there job, not mine, I was a patient, can't be my own doctor.

I did call my husband, my brother and I don't know who else probably I text or call. I had weakness and dizziness, no water or food for about four to five days. My husband told me that forget my assignment, "he knew that something major was happening in my mind" and he ask me to come home. I agree and wait the following Tuesday to call sick. Those hours I was the entire time looking for my brother and sister in law in the hotel, no success, they weren't never there. I already had a flight book in less than 24 hours. My question was? Can I be able to drive? I want someone taking me to the airport, but no one was with me.

In the hotel I start packing and praying for a safe driving to the airport. I was more concern about hurt someone with the car that mine on safety. That night was the one that I really feel that my brain was almost at the end. I knew that I lost control of my brain. I gave up. I was seen ghosts in my front yard in NY. I think that I called my husband, I was seen them through the home security that we have in our house. I even took pictures of them. Again I know now that I was having visual hallucinations.

My flight was around two PM and for reasons with no sense I start driving very early in the morning. Was about 6 AM that I get to the return of rental cars. Was in the opposite way of the airport, was a chaotic moment. Picture a petite woman carrying heavy luggage and try to get a shuttle for the airport, listening voices, talking to itself and to people created in her mind. Finally, I got to the airport, knowing that my mind was outer space. Did my family realized that I needed company, that I was begging for help? I guess never told them, again I am pretty good hiding my reality and feelings.

I realized that I was a woman reduced to a single instinct, Survival until I get home.

Okay, I was in the airport still thinking how he dare to leave me alone, I went early to the airport because I wanted to escape. Perhaps remember by that time I already hit the bottom, what was happening to me? I call Mike and he was surprise that I was too early in the airport, and I asked him where he was, but never had a clear answer, in my mind I understood that a friend flew him back to NY, I remember telling him that I didn't believed, but did I really call? I was still having doubts about who has being with me in Arizona, because I see them, talk to them but never face to face.

Dragging my luggage through the airport was exhausting, I got to the airline and was another disappointment, I was too early, couldn't check in. I guess have to wait about 3 to 4 hours to check in and being relieved from the luggage. Just remember my lectors my mind was not right, still was feeling confused, cloudy and foggy. I knew that I was by my own. I needed to hide my madness.

I call again my family, probably in a way they make me feel safe? Don't remember conversations but I was seen the nets all over the airport. I think that I talked with some people about if they were seen what I was experienced. Did they say yes? Don't recall. The entire time I was listening voices, from Mike, Jim and others members of the family. Jim was a friend of my husband, Mike that by my judgment was the one that invite him to participate in that strange "party "He was real in the real life. Always have not good sense from him. Perhaps that's why he was part of my insanity world.

I was listening everything that they were talking. Mike asked Joe if he can send the chopper to pick me up. I wouldn't catch his answer. In my mind never mind, I was lost. I decide to make the best of my horrific situation. I place the ear buds and start listening music and occasionally dancing. Can you picture that scenario my dear friends? I now remember that I heard my nieces talking about me, they were saying, that's my auntic always dancing and singing. That's was sweet, at least me dealing with my disturbed mind was like seen a rainbow In a cloudy day.

That day was probably the longest day in my life. I was wandering in the airport and all my senses were sharper than ever. I could hear what people were saying, or at least I thought. At the same time my family were doing arrangements with the airlines and airports so I will be taking the right plane. I knew I was confused but could not explain how. I knew in my mind that my brothers and my husband were watching me, they were telling me to get something to eat, and I did or I didn't? Remember that I always was looking up to try to find them; but they keep disappearing, what was happening?

When I pass the security, looking for the gate was an effort, I do remember that I called again my family, somehow I knew they were helping me. Mike, my husband told me that a doctor clears me to get in the plane, I don't recall, my mind was blocked, trapped, confuse. I do remember talking with people while waiting for boarding. I asked them if they see what I was seeing. Some of them told me that yes that those nets games have to be prohibit in public places, I agree and almost called them. I don't know if I did. Between the voices on my head and my surreal people perhaps I was not sure about nothing.

Finally, they start boarding the plane, I was one of the first they brought a wheelchair. I was feeling embarrassed, but I knew that my family made those arrangements for me. I heard people in the room saying that I was taking advantage, those comments make feel awful, but deep inside I wasn't me, feels like I was possessed by an unrealistic world created by the deepest memories of my lifetime? Or perhaps was just a way to cope from life. Was like a lifecycle, on and off, It's that's the way that the brain shutdown when you feel pain in your soul and you know that there's nothing or no one that can help you, pulling you out of the big black hole that was growing fast?

I was already seated in the plane. Well I am lying, that person was not me, was created by unknown circumstances, that person was experiencing the other side of the normalcy, already cross the line from sanity to insanity. What I am going to write now was unbelievable, but really was happening, I mean in my thoughts, was so real. The plane had a delay, I don't remember how long, meanwhile I started hearing voices this time some of them were not recognize by me, but others were very well known by me. They brought old memories from my childhood.

For you my readers understand my mysterious and vivid mental experience that I had in the plane I will share with you part of it. I was raised in a small town, walking distance to the shore. Very traditional, in which we all knew the locals. During holidays we all celebrate in the middle ot the town the specific day, during the festivals we use to dressed accordance with the celebration. I remember very well that during the holy week we dressed mimicking the suffering and sacrifice of Jesus. We celebrate almost all the festivals, and again always dressed accordance to the holiday.

Well, now going back to the plane, the voices were telling me about the Glory of God, was the Holy Week that we were celebrating in my confusion. I was hearing songs and Psalms that I recognize and knew. So in my mind I create a scenario, and those people closed to me were the actors and actresses. I know sound very weird but in my mind was so real. We were taking videos and capturing pictures all the time I knew that something was wrong, deep inside I was frightened. The actors were changing costumes; we create or just me? A theater, well kind of, I recognized voices of peoples from my town, they were in the same mindset that I was, again everything was created and was so real, whal is happening with my brain? Actually I enjoy that part of my madness, we or I had a mission, spread the Christianity to others. I had a gentleman in the center seat that what I recall, he was telling me stories from the old days, I think he was just showing some kindness and compassion, did he catchup that I was crazy? This flight to Baltimore was long and complicated, very confused. I was lost again this time I was living a different life, went back to the past, to my childhood.

I remember that some people were saying that we can be sued, because my entire crew was also taking pictures, the problem was that we didn't ask permission to do it. How much was real I don't know, everything through my eyes was true, so vivid and clear. We decide while still in the plane to share the pictures and phone numbers to protect each other in case of a legal problem and edit all pictures and videos to share with others, like in a theater. I don't remember if we did it.

The departure of my next plane was so closed to the landing, can someone, anyone help me? I ran to catch the plane, I needed to go home. They wait for some of us, because of the delay that we had in Phoenix, finally I was on my way home. However, I create another story. This time I was seen people looking at me and talking about drugs, I was very scared because I don't use them, and much less carrying them. I was paranoid, saw the police always looking at me and mysterious mind the stewardesses were always trying to get in my bag looking for drugs. I saw the police and strange persons always watching me, they were all over, while flying I remember seen them in the roof of the plane, very odd but that was happening in my reality; was a nightmare or never happened? Was a relief when the plane land, however I didn't know if the police will be waiting for me in Albany. My paranoia was getting worsened.

I don't recall nothing what happened in the airport, I just wanted to go home. I don't remember when I saw my husband, I do remember though that I told him something about drugs and that I was watched. His face was calm but something was wrong, I was feeling it. We get inside the car, in the back seats, my stepson was driving; and immediately I saw a girl in the passenger seat, I asked him if she was his friend, but she keep disappearing, I started seen nets again. I was furious because I thought that they were playing games with me. After that I saw my husband talking in his cell, he was talking with my brother, they wanted to take me to the hospital, I was refusing and yelling at them, I was beyond tears; finally, they convinced me to go to emergency room, I told them that just for few hours, was night time,

I was exhausted inside and outside; I was mad at them definitely they are not taking me home. They were driving to the hospital. I didn't want to go, I want to see my house, my dog, but they didn't listen. I think that I talk with my brother and he convinced me to go to emergency room, he calms me down for few minutes. Meanwhile I was in the car feeling frighten, a car was following us, what is what they want from me?

In my delusions, everybody had a conspiracy against me. Why this is happening? Why they are after me? I kept saying to my husband that he needs to see my back pack and my purse and hide everything from them, actually was nothing to hide, I was perhaps hiding myself from reality, from the darkness from my nightmare.

I was feeling confused and disturbed, the voices never stop and I was seen people that were just in my mind. The emergency room was a nightmare for me, I saw all my brothers and nieces, actually my entire family. They were talking about me at the beginning in the hallways, I was feeling embarrassed and I think that I start hating the place, I was screaming at nothing. They gave us a private room. I remember calling my daughter, but she was part of my imagination. I wanted to see my son, but everything was happening so fast that I then completely loose it.

I don't remember too much in the emergency room. I did hear over and over the same question; do you drink or use any type of drugs. My husband response was always no, same response as mine. They were concerned that probably in Arizona someone pours a hallucinogen substance in my glass or if I ate mushrooms. I understood their concern but I couldn't see how that might happen. Please release me, let me go.

I do remember the doctor, was a female? She was very patient and sweet. After that all the memories were block. I went in a catatonic state for about 6 hours, I was told by my family. Just imagine the impression and the shock that they went through, they were dealing with a different person through all that nightmare. Picture someone that you love in a fetal position, immobile with doing involuntary movements, frightening ah.

When I wake up? What is happening, set me free, I beg you., I don't remember if I was still in the emergency room or in the room. I was very confused, still with visual and hearing hallucinations. I do remember that I was feeling more and more furious because I wanted to be in my house. I will summary my behavior, Out of Control. I know now that my family and my husband were in contact during the entire time.

My husband told me that a good friend came to emergency room while I was in the catatonic state. He prayed for me; I do remember having aa holly rosary in my hands, never asked how, who or when I got it. I was waiting for my brother and sister in law, (for respect to them I will change their names, Ed and Jen.) They were with me in Arizona, remember that I was looking for them, they were like my helpers. I remember that I called Ed and explained my mysterious and strange encounters with the nets and I do remember that he calms me down, he was always with me through my mysterious illness even when he was not there in real life. I wanted badly his presence to be there for me. But again all delusions.

I remember the tears of my husband but I was unable to comfort him. Everything was unbelievable and unpredictable. I was in my own world, probably taking a break from LIFE. I realized that I pray a lot to have that break. It was happening and deep inside I wanted to escape from that nightmare or break from life. I can't run, can't escape Many persons came to draw blood or to take me to have a lot of imaging tests. Not one-time one of them told me what they are going to be doing on me, perhaps I don't remember, my brain that was spinning never shutdown, I was feeling confused, wasted, drained and scared to death. How long I was out, don't know and probably refused to know, was too scary.

My paranoia didn't stop, got worse in the hospital. I couldn't trust in no one. I was seen and hearing bad things, all about me. They were trapping me, I wanted to run away. I think that I try to tell my family about my paranoid thoughts, but they didn't believed me. How long pass already? What is happening to me? I have to fight this but how, I was sick, mentally ill. I know that. Time tor me to start healing. Do I will have the strength? Doctors and nurses were always in and out from my room. My husband looks devastated, nothing that I can do to help him.

Finally, Ed and Jen came, they were in Florida and took a plane to be there with me. I still remember his faces, they look sad and scared. They tried to explain why I was in the hospital. They have to understand that I want to go home, I came from the airport to a hospital, I needed to understand that I was really sick. My situation was serious. Oh my GOD help me. I need to start trusting again, that has to be the first step otherwise I will never be me the woman that is now reduced to bones, my weight was in the seventy pounds. My mind was blocked to reality. I was trapped. I need to start saying that I don't hear voices or see things anymore, otherwise I will be in the hospital forever.

I don't remember when my son came, but I do know that because of that nightmare, I started fighting for my sanity, that moment mark the fight that I just me can battle, was for me imperious to get better, I don't want him to suffer. His name Fred, he meant a lot to me. He flew from Jersey to be with me, even that I knew I was withdrawn from real life I have the willing to come back from the underground that I was for who knows how long. Seen my husband and my family makes me stronger. This can't defeat me. Definitely this will not brake me. Everything seems unreal, I have to re-embrace again with the reality.

I was admitted six long days in the hospital, unable to sleep, and desperate to be discharge. I believed that the doctors didn't know how to handle my paranoid psychosis. My life jumped from be functional to be completely insane. Gradually I started hearing less voices and seen less imaginary people. I needed to go home, please, give me the opportunity to reborn in my own environment. Finally, I was discharge, still feeling cloudy and foggy. They told me that was normal and gradually they expect less symptoms.

We went home, Fred my son took some time off to be with me. I was weak and dizzy; I was literally almost bedridden for six days. Gradually started doing simple things in the house I think help me gain strength. I start eating, which was very important for my recovery. The family went back to their own routines. I was feeling more normal, still foggy though. One day I took my phone to see the ghosts that I was seen while I was in Arizona, also I wanted to see the pictures and videos taken in the plane. Was a scary moment because until that day everything was very abstract, now I have evidence. There are no pictures no video no ghosts, all that I saw was dark and the videos just me talking with myself. I know now that I was **trapped in my mind**.

My lesson from this mental break down still unknown. If this might happen again, unpredictable as the doctors said. If I am scared, yes, don't know how will be tomorrow or more frightening in the next second. For now I lived day by day, knowing that we are so weak and that **tomorrow is unknown.**

I am a woman just coming out from an acute psychotic episode. I was feeling confused and now I feel concern about my future. There are too many uncertainties, will this nightmare will become a recurring episode in my life? It's a mystery, No person can give me a straight answer. I am trying to move forward, and most important, need to convince myself that will never reoccur. It's suppose that I have to avoid stress, confrontations and problems to prevent another event, yeah right. Life is full of those. That's why I decide to write and vent my emotions and feelings before they get on me.

For you my lectors that for whatever reason been in that mysterious world that I was, believed in yourself, use all your power and fight, just remember and I quote: what doesn't brake you make you stronger. I will continue keep in touch with you, meanwhile hang in there. This short book it's written in a way that might be hard to understand, but I still feel cloudy. No more hallucinations but after my brainstorm the thought process has being hurt in some inexplicable way.

Now has been a month since I get home and I have to learn how to deal and understand the aftermath. Will not be easy that's a fact, however I will learn again how to recover my mechanism of defense to cope with the daily situations in life. I been thinking about that mental episode, what generate and trigger it? Might be a combination of factors that cause the carrousel inside of my brain. What scare me the most is; what if happens again. I don't want to see those nets never again. Was very disturbing and I am afraid that probably next time I will not come out.

Life is a cycle, everything comes in episodes, back and forth. You don't know what might happen in the near future, no ones knows, perhaps the answer it's unknown even for the doctors, they cannot give you a clear answer. I am living day by day, trying to make the best of each day, but honestly it's difficult.

I am going back in my life trying to put the puzzle together and I realized that my mind never shutdown since I was a child, always speeding, night and day, even my sleep deprivation has been abnormal in the last ten years. I knew was not right but no time to think in my health. I guess that the healing process will be longer that I thought. Can't escape from my reality, I was sick, very ill and the paranoia and the psychosis indeed happened. I am grateful that in my crisis didn't hurt no one (while driving) and also I was lucky that I was not hurt, I meant physically.

I have to think every day like it's the first day of my life, not the last one. Perhaps I have to make changes in my life to prevent stressful situations and learn again to regain peace inside of me, nobody can do it just me. Will be a difficult path but I don't have choices. I can't go backwards; I will not have another mental break down. I am willing to learn more about how to live with myself and my surroundings, wherever it take.

I REFUSE TO BE TRAPPED ON MY MIND AGAIN, I AM A SURVIVAL AND I HAVE TO REMEMBER THAT I ESCAPE FROM THE INSANITY AND RETURNED TO THE WORLD, LIKED OR NOT.

I will give you some advice how to hold and keep your mind clear. How to avoid to be predisposed to lose your mind. I will share with you part of my life, which I think that have some importance in my mental health. I used to live in a log cabin, was around 2005, in the woods with 43 acres, very quiet place. By that time my husband was traveling as usual. My brother Alf came to visit me, that was in 2006 and I remember these words. We were in the porch, he looks at me and made this comment looking at my face, and I quote: these place is beautiful but be careful, too much solitude will get to you, might trick your mind.

Probably that was the beginning of my nightmare, who knows, but indeed he was right. I start with insomnia, and always looking if something happens I needed to protect myself. My neighbors were apart from my house. The one across the street was an insecure and noisy woman with an evil heart. Always trying to help me in some way, I try to ignore them, please respect the boundaries that were already in place. Was also a very disturbing time of my life.

She, (don't recall her name) was every time trespassing into my property, for what reason? Never knew never care. But I do remember many nights I tried to avoid her as much as I can, but she knew my routine in a daily basis. I was about one hour from my job. During winter took me longer to get to the job, Icy roads, deer's, plenty of snow. I was okay with that. Meanwhile my neighbor across the road was playing filthy games with me. In my land I had expensive tiles and equipment I. She used to put a sign in my property that said take it is free. That made me mad and the police told me to do whatever is necessary to protect myself and my property. They were snowing nights that I was hidden waiting for her, let me clear some of these were very real; was not paranoia, was living a nightmare while awake. Needed to get out of that mountain, needed my freedom my space.

I decide to move out from my piece of mountain, couldn't take that anymore. For about 11months I move to an apartment, which didn't last I was not used to live surround of noises. By that time, I was looking for a place to live. I found a place closed to my job but at the same time in the woods. I loved it, but again loneliness and solitude. I was dealing at the same time with breast cancer for two years, surgery after surgery,

I managed well or I thought I did, don't know now. After my episode of psychosis, I started having doubts about everything. After couple of years living in that beautiful place; I moved again, this time out of state, Florida. I decided to give a chance, was a beautiful home that my husband bought for me. But I was alone with my dog. My neighbors were amazing, good people and she, her name Col was my savior. I was giving up on life; Now that I am looking back I did had a nervous breakdown due many negative factors that were happening in my life by those days.

My husband seems to not understand my situation or was in denial. After a year and a half my neighbor call him, and told him that I was falling apart, no eating, no sleep no life, he decided to come home due my status, I was not doing well. In my job I was doing well don't know how, push myself through the edge, I started falling apart inside and outside. Waking up in the morning was a challenge, I was at that point completely broken; pieces of me all over, some missing, some lost forever. That was the beginning of the end. The end of my sanity, I was too closed to that fine line.

Please need help want to stay in this side of the world. In the world that I can function, let me rephrase in the world that I can use a mask to hide my me. Everything was chaos couldn't stand working with corporations that just care about money, working long hours. Husband that was absent under the same roof. I try many times to find him, but he was a stranger, didn't recognized this new man. Didn't know what to do, choices, choices, never was good in that.

I was feeling the same with and without him, our lives drifted apart, big time what should I do? I don't want to be hurt anymore, walk away or not. I am at this point on my life that don't care. I felt many times to ran away and don't look back. But we talked about start from scratch again, do I want that, unknown, too much uncertainty, I resign my job and again thinking about moving. I was not sure about nothing anymore, I was mentally exhausted, I exceed the limits, I will follow the flow.

Then we moved to North Carolina, another nightmare, he moved first. Meanwhile I was living in our boat, was different and interesting. The waves used to wake me up, I was different by that time, trying to enjoy, whatever that means. NC didn't last either. They promised that he will be home every night but that was not the case. We then moved back to Florida and in less than three months to South Africa. That didn't last either for many reasons that one day I will share with you my lectors.

As soon we return to Florida, we discussed and decide to went back home, NY. I drove to NY looking for a job and housing. Was not a pleasant journey, I was bouncing between interviews and looking for houses with my friend Lola, she was our realtor, but no success. That road trip gave me bad taste; my senses were telling me that something wasn't right, but I did drove back to Florida with several contracts on my hands. I choose the one I thought was the best for me. We then moved to a rental house while my husband was looking to buy a house.

Finally, we found a place closed to a lake in the woods. I choose that house. Another chaos, another bad choice the place that I started working was impossible due intimidation and discrimination, but I did my best with no regrets. I was driving about one hour in good weather. I resigned after 16 months of literally speaking hell, meanwhile by those months my husband always looking for jobs, went to Panama. I was answering recruiters' offers, and that's when I decide start doing Locums in different states.

The job in Panama didn't work, so I knew that I had to work, I already compromised myself to work out of state. After all this odyssey you already knows what happened. The lesson that I have to share with others is, we need stability, peaceful environment and most important avoid too much solitude, Alf, you were right, the loneliness and the instability got on me. Please live stable with peace in your heart and mind. Eat healthy, sleep well, don't hesitate to ask for help. Don't feel ashamed it is what it is. Have good friends and be thankful every day for what you have and don't have, trust me there is a reason.

Now my life change will be a long and probably hard process, but my faith will give me the strength and the resources for a complete healing. It's like a reborn anyway what meant to be meant to be, I am now in baby steps, healing inside and outside. Will not be an easy journey, but much better than before. While I was writing I got more concern, apparently going back in my life made me acknowledged that I had a mild episode of nervous breakdown while living in Florida; not as bad like this recent event, but that might mean that I am predisposed. This can have recurred at any moment and probably worse. I have to tell this episode to my psychiatrist, it's very important, because the prognosis would change.

The strong woman that I thought I was disappeared, doesn't exist was deleted by some higher power; I am just a very susceptible person with an uncertain future that vanished, that frightening me, but no matter what I will be calm and think positive, will be a long unpredictable road. Not easy but it's worthy because might make a difference between me staying in the sane side or cross forever the fine line between sanity and insanity, I don't want to stay in the cloud and this confusing world. I will keep fighting, anyhow at the end will be what will be.

My tomorrow is in my hands, I have to work hard from me, myself and I. Everything and nothing matters anymore. Happiness, tranquility and peace are on me. Do I be able to handle the uncertainty, the unknown? There are no answers, it's just day by day. I want to thanks my husband, my son, my brothers, sister in law and friends that were on my side while I was battling my insanity. Love you all.

My husband and family was really worried about me, I knew that at the end, I couldn't described how insane I was , I do know that everything in my mind was real perhaps in the real world wasn't. Or indeed was happening, I will never know, neither you.

THE END

DECISIONS

To trust or let it go, to live or choose to just exist
No questions, no answers
Stay alive or choose too just quit
The brain choose not to answer

Choices, choices, challenges, challenges
Did I have it right or not?
Decide to exceed my power to be happy
Decide to fight for the freedom and linger my mind

Smell the roses, kiss the soil
Ride a horse and enjoy the ride
No more why's No more questions
Just kiss yourself and love yourself

Stay still and stare at stars
Stay still and make a wish
No more questions waiting for answers
Just there waiting for grace and greats.

Nothing happens for a reason
Everything happens for a reason
Just look up and beyond
Faith and everything will go around

Around what? Never mind
All what counts it's the rain,
The sky, the fall, the laugh and kind
Keep it quiet and never mind.

Life needs inspiration and what you do with that can change
How you go about living.
Fueling life that will put you into motivation to get the most on
your lifetime
Be creative, be passionate be you..

Broke never, fight until your last breath
At the end will be what will be
Good or bad you won
Swim, feel the waves and life will turn out how will turn out
Be grateful or not that's a choice
Be you not what people want you to be
No tears or tears, laugh or not laugh
Inspired yourself for just you and that will create a
New you, better you, smarter and wiser . That's the clue of living
With and without tearing
With and without laughing.

Tired to carry heavy luggage
wind take away from me what I don't need
Everything that don't let me move on
Just want to carry what fit in my pocket and my heart.

Has to be a way, but which way ?
Feel release but how ?
Feeling heavy, tight
Wind protect my mind.

Promises, lies, nothing matter will be what will be
Moving forward or backwards it's the same.

Luz Pratt

Choices, hope, nothing matters
Stop or continuing nothing matter, the unknown
Will be the same.,because at the end will be what will be .

Being able to breath it's a gift
Being able to love
Feeling the air in your lungs
And not grasping for her it's a gift

Having thoughts without having them
Feeling empty knowing the answers.

Making love in your mind,no one with you
Smiling to nothing and crying for everything

Be able to absorb the reality surround you
Without not having it.
Life change so fast that make it impossible
To keep up with the flow
Carrying a heavy luggage when you
Know it's empty, having the feeling of drowning
In the deepest place, unknown.

Everything must go or
Everything must stay
You know the answer
Then go as a feather
Smooth, quiet
Fly, rest, don't look back
Don't look forward
Don't look at all
At the end it's everything or nothing

There is something magic about fall
The red, yellow and orange leaves

Trees shouting out loud the Glory of God
Nature giving their beauty with no expectations.

Life is full of beauty and sorrows
No time to complaint,no one listen
Life is full of things and emptiness
No time to complaint, everybody listen.

Yesterday I had a dream, a dream of love
The love that never exist
Yesterday I had a dream, you were in my dreams
So far and so close that I try many times to touch you

Did I? Was a sweet sensation, so real that I did not want to
wake up
We were just together,staring at each other
Talking about the future, the past, the present

We did have a very complicated past but full of love

We do not have a today, was just a dream
We talk about our tomorrow,the uncertain future.
When you walk in my life many years ago
I was a young girl with expectations of happiness
I want to continue pursuing it, but drift so far from me
Even our future will be complicated, or not?

Half of my life has been, dreaming about
What if? But again the reality is now, you are not here
You are not there
Don't want to face it anymore
Don't want to love you anymore.

The fall always bring memories
Memories that are inbreed in my blood

Luz Pratt

Memories that are yellow,orange and red
Like the fall in my place

What if? Did I or We ever got an answer ?
Unknown
What if? If I say yes,will change something
Or nothing?

We all know destiny, can she answer me back
We still have a chance or not
When the time pass,never comes back
Do we still have a chance or not …

Yesterday I had a dream … …
Today I remember the dream
Tomorrow, no one knows
Can I live in my dream?

Eternal moments, sweet and passionate
Days staring at the window, waiting and waiting
I know in my heart that some one above control
Everything, my Lord do I have the right to keep waiting

Now the reality, nor you in my day
Now the guilt, the tears
My day today like every other day
With you but without you, with love but not love

Ghosts that follow me, where ever I go
Reality that got lost
Ghosts from my past,my present
Future that doesn't exist.

Difficult times in life, then fly, like an eagle
as higher as you can, fast and far

That way you don't have to hide
just get away from the stormy days.

Just when you feel you are alone
Breath, smile,touch
Nothing to fear
Run,and follow the ride

Secrets,just for me
Don't want to sale my freedom
Lies, never for me
Don't want to live, that hurts.

Forgive it's a decision that just you can make
Forget,never stay tucked in your heart
Trust, hard to put in pieces
What get broke,can't be unbroken .

Too much luggage,let it go
Too heavy, I am drowning
Need to throw things,forgive
Need to do it, let it go.

Forgiveness it's a decision, not a feeling,
It's a choice that you make
Because that hate that you carry in your
Heart it's heavier than you think

Unable to move on, unable to stay either
Decisions, decisions
Can't reach the mountain
Can't swim the lake, much less the occan.

Just let if go
Something better will come

Just let it go
Something profound will come.
Poems Written by the Author:

Life test you, too many tricks,too many of everything
Too much of deception,tears,choices.
Passing through life with the fear of every second
With the fear of knowing the unknown
Passing through life with emotions of every second
Expecting from each minute, just You

Big challenges that you need to accomplish
Deep and shallows, doesn't matter they are all the same
Daily challenges waiting for answers
Waiting for the unpredictable that happen.

Very simple nothing is the same, we rotate like the earth,
Depends of the moon and the sun the gravitation
Takes you deeper in your thoughts, that deep
That you can't find yourself .

Do I want to see my real me
Do I want to face myself
No it's too dark or yo brilliant
No let me be without knowing
Just let me be.

Holding thoughts that hurts
Holding thoughts that smile to the past
Passing through with deception and tears
Tears that no one sees, just You.

How much of energy I still got?
How much of everything?

And in the deepest part of my brain
Just waiting for what?

Too many years waiting, too many years
Rivers of tears
Rivers of tears
Too many years waiting,too many years.

Yesterday I had a dream we finally were together
Too disturbing, was not real
Yesterday I finally have you
Too complicated,was not real

Lightning a candle waiting to see reality
Waiting for answers
Waiting with tears
Lightning a candle wailing to see you, to see us.

Taking chances, like rolling dices
Not taking any
Everything is a myth
I will roll the dices again, waiting for luck
No luck just reality.

Hard to understand the present
Difficult to forget the past
Much more unpredictable with the future
Hardest to predict, don't want to know

No expectations will be easier
Then no deception
No expectations will be hard
Then no hope, no light,no peace

Luz Pratt

What will be the best way to live in this
Unpredictable lifetime
Just seat, smell the rain
Thank for everything
Thanks for nothing.

Everything is easy to say but hard to follow
Pursuing happiness,love,peace
Earth do you remember that I live here
Do you remember my dreams and goals

No you don't, you go so fast, hard to catch up
But yes you know, I know you do
Perhaps everything is in my head
Perhaps this is the way that supposed meant to be.

More questions, more concerns
Leave me alone, please
Shut down my brain,don't want to think,don't want to expect.
Perceptions and dreams,are they the same
They overlap in my head and heart
Like a big wave,with a large current
That brake in the shore but doesn't stay.

The current taking me to the deepest part, between the waves
I can't see nothing, can't breath
I need to get out of this rip
Can't breath, please help

Not easy to live, not easy to die
It's a puzzle that never finish
It's a puzzle with missing pieces
Not easy to live, not easy to die.

The Clift is too high and profound
The thoughts are too intense and deep
No nothing and everything
Just me, my thoughts and the pain.

Pain all over inside and outside,
Waiting for the reality to surface
Hurt all over, broken heart
Unable to save, unable to rise.

Give me the peace, give me the serenity
Take away my sorrows
Give me the love and embrace me
Take away my ignorance

Yes ignorance of the truth, the real truth
Ignorance of living
Give me wisdom to understand the
Understandable and the strength for
Keep going between the dark and the light.

The dark is not that black
The light is not that bright
Whatever it is
Want to see,want to know.

I did had a strange dream, you, me and my past
I try to make it true, didn't happen
I want u so bad, that serious that if I can change
In my lifetime or at least cut pieces of them,probably and I say
Probably the dream will come true .

I am kidding myself again, mind stop wandering
Mind stop dreaming

Luz Pratt

Nothing was real, never was
Just me and my voice begging for a change.

A change that will never happen
I feel ill in my heart
Feel strange,feel unique in my
Thoughts and feelings,are they real?

Want to go to another planet, I don't belong here
Want to be invisible so no one sees me
Please give my privacy back
Don't look for me, don't waste your time.

Don't want to be found
Don't want to be hurt
Give back my wings
Give back my peace.

Decisions,choices, overall that's life
Didn't have choices but indeed took
Decisions that I regret or not, not sure
Both together make me who I am now
A free spirit that can't find the way home.

The way home, where is home?
It's all over,want to belong to something
No way in no way out
Just deeper and deeper.

Not expecting answers or solutions
Just here taking my inside to the outside
Just here in my solitude
Waiting for a light showing me the road back.

Can't win its too strong, can't win its to intense
Trapped in my own decisions no other choices
Want to win though, want to be me again
Want to go home,do you hear me? Wants to go home
Whenever place is.

Don't whisper to me, can't hear
Talk loud and I will follow
Can't see, be my eyes
don't want to miss the road again.

My love can't find you,are you lost like me
My life can't see it, are you blind like me
Need answers, need to recover my brain
Need to reinstall my life to day one.

If there is just a possibility of do that
I will take it
Can't do it anymore, feel weak
I surrender, please forgive me and guide me

No energy, feel drain,wasted worthless
Knowing the unknown
Will be the first part of my cure
Will be the first step, the first sign of strength .

Waiting for that moment feels forever
Feels sometime impossible
Waiting for that moment ...
Then I will take the wheels and start before the beginning
Before the ending.

Fire in my brain, need water
Fire in my soul, need peace

Don't see answers, can't hear them
Don't see the beginning until the end.

Want to fight negativism, hard to do it
Want to fly like a bird and disappear
No need to be sad it's my decision
No need to look for me, don't want to be found.

Living in a place,that is not my place
Living and dying at once
No need for answers, was a choice
No need for nothing just write .

Giving myself to pages that can't be erased
Giving everything that I am to you
Receiving back more questions
Receiving back memories that want to erased?

No please don't erase the only thing that it's left
My memoirs
No please don't erase them so I can learn
From them,not sure what I want . Please pain go away.

Can't think properly it's a roundabout
That keep taking me to the same place
Over and over, no escape, no exit seen
Trapped in my own thoughts, in my own life.

Did you ever feel the same or its just me
Did you ever feel lost, no way to go
I did and I am, can't find the way to go back
Can't find the road,can't find the road.

Hopeless and loneliness are two factors
Facts that stopped me to move on

Facts that don't allow peace inside, I become part
Of my own destiny without asking me.

Deception, disappointment,
Faith and hope
Both walk together
Both with me all the time

Too many clouds, darkness
Too much hope, brightness
Which one will come first? That will be the answer.
No need to be with people to figure somethings out
No need to be alone
No need to be in solitude or sadness
Just need light,guidance for my way to go home.

Home is my past, home is where my heart used to be
Home is family, but where are they?
Oh my Lord give me your wisdom, let my fight
I am blind but I can see people in the way they really are not
in the way
They want us to see them .

I am here please don't forget me
It's like dying
I am here don't abandon me
I keep trying.

It's a cycle, no matter what I see or go
It's the same
It's a vicious cycle, and the big ball
Bring you to the same place, no way to go.

I had a dream, a dream about you, yes you know who
We finally met after almost 40 years

Luz Pratt

Do you remember, I don't I keep loosing my mind over and
over
Long time ago, too many lost years.

Are you with me or I am with you?
Don't know there is not us
Silence and solitude
Silence within us, within our blood

Big ocean of tears, detach of reality
No caring, no passion
No point of return
No point what's going on around you

I fly alone, I climb alone
Having strong wings
Make me go higher and higher
Because I fly alone have strongest wings.

The power of love is greater than anything else
The love of power is strong but selfish
Write in your heart everything that matters
Keep in your mind everything that counts.

It's not possible give love with an empty heart
It's possible give love if you got it
The today feels numb, no feelings
Just fly in the cyclone and follow the winds.

Are you with me or not
Life are you?
Are you with me or not
Death are you?

Give your power to others
Give me your power to finish
Don't do it, will be selfish
You do it I will be grateful

Grateful of knowing that I am not alone
Grateful of what?
No one is here, no one
Only the dark space, no light for me, for us?

The church can tell some stories that I kept hidden
No need to ask me just go and listen
Places that if they can talk
Will tell you my sins, my real inside.

I lost track of time and all my dreams flew far away
Before came all true
Pursue them don't lost them
They will never come back, they flew fast and I am lost.

I have to allow that the strength of love reborn on me
I need the tools, I need the instructions
Want to change the world, or simply
Want to change my thoughts. Need to change this new me.

Everything it's a random, happiness, sadness, joy, madness
Nothing get resolved though
Getting closed to reality, scary, don't know what to expect
I want everything gone, I want everything back, very bizarre

But that's my life, my insight never shut down
Never give up even-though I do to get some relief from my brain
No questions ask neither questions
Just let me take a deep breath and fight with the unfight.

Too much to think, too much hurt
Need a break for restart my me,
Need a break to breath and feel
Too much to to forget, not in me, though

If I just can reset myself, if that will help
Who knows, again the unknown
If I just can undo what was done
Perhaps I might live in my life.

At present I am not living, I am just here
Can't take no more
Choose to have a death while living
Choose to survive, decisions,decIsions ...

Trust that's a no, neither forgive
Being here without my presence
I am obsolete, don't count
Being just with my shadow that don't recognized anymore.

Mind sleeping, thoughts confuse, mouth shut

Which world I am at, need to release myself from me

Awkward moment in my life, don't know how to go back .

Go back where? Go back for what? No matter what; life is shut.

I can see me at the bottom of the sea, staring at the darkness
of the moment, enjoying the loneliness inside of my solitude.
Don't remember the brightest of life perhaps there is no life
anymore or better yet

Probably the ocean it's all what I got now, showing me the Glory of the Nature so I can wake up from this nightmare that is swallowing my soul, my feelings, my dreams.

However I want to get out I want to know me again. Start a new life with my old me, this new me is trapped and I used to be a free spirit, now I am just these; a couple of words encrypted in a piece of paper with no beginning no end.

Seen clouds through the clarity of the water, thirty feet under and thirty feet above . Unable to perform, unable to think straight due the dark inside my mind. Can I clear it can you clear it for me? Or this is just another weird thought. Can't remember, help me remember please . My entire life went upside down and I am lost.

I am going to fight it, alone as always but with company at the same time, me and myself, I trust my cognitive, I trust my mind even though doesn't belong to me anymore, I am a stranger inside of me, oh well, Faith keep me going, Faith in the highest,, Faith in my instincts.Faith in reality.

Today I wake up with something, with memories when all this started, with memories that frighten me, don't want to, don't let me go again. Rescue is on their way; for whom, for me ? For you? Again unknown. Too much mystery, too much uncertainty, just let me be, let me go.

No need for pity, need to fight It therefore stay with me and follow my path, follow my madness, will see at the end the outcome, unpredictability, loosing my mind and find it again . Fine line between the unreal and the presently chaos.

Everything is falling apart or is just destiny? Be with me all the way, don't abandon me don't give up on me. I need your strength, your peace, need to cross back that fine line that is keeping me stuck, trapped. Don't want to be alone in this horrific road that started too long ago and I can't stopped.

Feelings, love, hate, scary things, don't want to be alone

Thought about you, why ? Don't know, probably perhaps don't want to stay trapped, don't want to be stuck.

Live without living, dying without die, love with no love, that's all what's is about, questions with no answers. You all at least response one, be with me, want to run and never stop, running and running just to get to that place for return from the unreturned. Not easy, no guarantees just hope, just hope.

Being myself without being me, sound sad? Incredible? But fighting is the only choice that I can see in my today my tomorrow. Karma? No, everything is in my head, or nothing is in there, don't know, don't care, for what ? My present is empty, no memoirs, nothing to grab, nothing to remember.

Need to reopen everything to find my last chapter, need to figure out how everything started and perhaps how everything will ended, for what? and why?

Need to know, might be the only way that I can closed it and moved in to the reality, just to be in, just to be me again without nightmares and madness in my mind.

AUTHOR BIOGRAPHY

I am a 58 years old, female medical doctor, remarried now, slim and very outgoing. My life was raising my kids, been mom, dad and provider for about 13 years, I was feeling by those days strong and many times weak at the same time, struggling a lot to make a living for my family. Literally I was working twenty-four seven days a year, living more in hospitals that in my house. Needed to be strong to survive. Never complaint in life you need to do whatever it takes to make it worth it, just living day by day in my precious island that is full of amazing memories with hidden secrets; then all change. By those years I was waiting for a phone call, waiting for few words;" I want you back", didn't happen. I knew that my children were at that age that needed me the most, days, weeks and time were passing fast. Did my best, give the most of me to my family and my career. Didn't realize that my inside was getting emptier, I was feeling there is nothing left. I remarried with a man that travel a lot due his career, he is a Project Manager, we have different careers with multiple responsibilities. I remember very well the promise that we made, that we will never live apart, no matter what. Promises never respected.

At present I am actively working as a Physician or I was. I have been very grateful with my job and always very conscious about the responsibility of my career. I love what I do for living, it's one of my passions, yes I have too much to give too much to love. I used to enjoy the outdoors, dancing and everything in a way that fulfills my days with energy. Since I was a kid I used to write here and there just for myself. This time I will share a deep experience that recently cross my road and probably change my life forever. This situation occurs about one month ago, May 2015.